Think About It, You
Might Learn Something

Also by ROBYN SUPRANER

Would You Rather Be a Tiger?

ROBYN SUPRANER

Think About It, You Might Learn Something

Illustrated by Sandy Kossin

HOUGHTON MIFFLIN COMPANY BOSTON

Library of Congress Cataloging in Publication Data

Supraner, Robyn.
  Think about it, you might learn something.

  SUMMARY: A fourth grader records in her diary
only those events which she considers most important
and thought provoking.

  (1. Humorous stories) I. Kossin, Sandy, illus.
II. Title.
PZ7.S9652Th   (Fic)   73-8752
ISBN 0-395-17707-3

To all children, everywhere,
because they have possibilities

Think About It, You
Might Learn Something

1

THIS IS NOT a diary. First of all, I'm only going to tell about important things. Not like how I washed my hair and polished my nails, or how I put some new kind of perfume behind my ears. That's the kind of stuff Julie's sister writes in her diary. Her sister is fifteen and, if you ask me, she has a pretty boring diary. I don't blame her for hiding it. Second of all, I'm not going to write stuff every day. Just when I feel like it.

My mother says that writing things down helps you sort them out. Once I had a fight with Julie and I wrote it down. When I read it, it was as if it didn't happen to me but to some other kid. I could tell right away that I should have punched her. That's probably what my mother means about sorting out.

My mother is always making lists, like what got messed up and has to be cleaned, or what she served to company so she won't serve the same thing twice. Personally, I think if it tasted good the first time, she should make it again. I could eat tuna fish on white bread, with plenty of mayonnaise, for breakfast, lunch, *and* dinner.

So far I can't think of anything to write. I guess when there's something to say, I'll know.

2

THIS IS a really dumb story. The only reason I'm telling it is because my mother said, "Think about it, you might learn something."

It was last Sunday and we were all getting ready to go to the beach except for Blooper, who takes up the whole back seat, and Snitch, who hates the beach anyway.

Chip, my little brother, was getting cookie all over his face for the five million trillionth time and my mother was starting to get upset. She kept saying, out loud, "It's nine-thirty. It's nine-thirty-five. It's nine-forty," like a regular cuckoo clock. My father was out in the car, leaning on the horn and hollering, "WHAT'S TAKING SO LONG? THE *##!!** TRAFFIC WILL BE BUMPER TO BUMPER! WHAT'S HOLDING UP THE SHOW?" Don't even ask me what *##!!** means. I would have to stay in my room for at least a week if I told you.

The thing that was holding up the show was my yellow bathing suit. The one with the red dots was still at Julie's and the orange one got ripped on Sparky Farentino's slide last Thursday. That boy is *so* stupid. My poor bathing suit is ripped to pieces and all he can say is "I can see your bee-hind! I can see your bee-hind!" What a baby! Anyway, that left the yellow one and I couldn't find it anywhere.

By this time Chipper, my little brother, was getting his face all messy with a green lollipop and my mother and father were *really* sounding upset, so I had to tell them about the bathing suit. Last Friday morning my mother said, "If you lose one more thing! If you lose *one* more thing!" When she says a thing twice, look out!

When I told her about my bathing suit, my mother looked up at the ceiling and said very quietly, "Did you look in your room?" Then she hollered out to my father, "SHE CAN'T FIND HER BATHING SUIT!"

My father took his hand off the horn and hollered back, through his teeth, "DID SHE LOOK CAREFULLY?" He really looks funny when he does that, but you should never laugh. Never.

I made a very serious face to show that I understand the value of a dollar.

"It's got to be *someplace*," my mother said. She always makes a big discovery out of something simple, but I didn't bother pointing that out to her.

"Let's look for it," my father said. We all stood in the middle of the living room, thinking where to look first. Then Potato Chip, my little brother, dragged out the box of sweaters and mittens that my mother had camphored away for the summer.

Sticking out of the corner was the yellow hat that used to match my rain slicker. I always wondered what happened to that hat. Blooper found our old percolator, which we don't need anymore because we got a new one, and Snitch found the feather from my father's new hat. Actually, he found the whole hat, but he found the feather first. There was no yellow bathing suit.

Then my mother marched into the bathroom

and we all followed. She opened the cabinet under the sink in a very fancy way. There were two forks, a plate with dried-up blueberry pie, a tangerine peel, some pits, and the bottoms of my winter pajamas. But no yellow bathing suit.

Next, we looked in the back hall closet. We found half a box of Cocoa Puffs, a bunch of my mother's fake curls, and Hickory and Dickory, my brother's pet mice who we thought had escaped.

My mother said, "My wiglet!"

My brother said, "My mice!"

My father said, "My God!"

And I said, "That still doesn't find my yellow bathing suit."

I would have been very happy to stop looking, right then and there. All that poking around wasn't doing much good, but my mother wouldn't give up.

We went upstairs. Mother tripped over Blooper and father stepped on Snitch's tail. Nobody said anything.

We found the turtle food and the turtle in the linen closet. We found three crunkled grapefruits, my father's striped tie, and Tony the Toad in Chipper's wardrobe. We found my mother's purple, *dyed-to-match* evening slippers under the daybed, and a lambchop bone and three thousand ants in Blooper's bed.

My mother got a headache. My father took two aspirins. But nobody found my yellow bathing suit.

Then Chipmunk, my little brother, started to giggle. He put his lollipop down on a good chair and pointed to Little Baby One Arm, my old doll. There, on her head, like a pair of earmuffs, was the top of my yellow bathing suit. Right that second, I remembered where

the bottom was. It was in my schoolbag. The one with the missing strap.

It took me about five seconds to get ready. I had to sit and wait for everyone.

The whole day wasn't spoiled. By two o'clock we found a good parking space and the old Chipadee had strawberry ice cream all over his face.

The beach was really great. I found my green knee socks rolled up in my bathing cap, and I found a million fantastic shells to take home.

Chiperoo, my little brother, only got lost once; and by the time we were ready to go home everyone was smiling, even though we never did find the blue shovel.

Well, that's all. I told you it was a dumb story. But my mother was right. I learned something. I learned that a person needs at least four bathing suits, or she's in bad trouble!

3

THE FIRST THING I want to say is that it wasn't my fault. The whole thing happened because Charles, my *baby* brother (you can tell I'm mad when I call him Charles) decided to be cute.

Anyway, Charles had this little green snake that looked and felt exactly like a real snake. It gave me the creepy-crawlies every time I saw it, so, naturally, he was always putting it in my schoolbag or in my bath or in some dumb place like that.

I'm usually not afraid of anything. I mean, who do you think picks up spiders by one leg and carries them outside when my mother starts screaming? Me. That's who. Spiders don't bother me one bit. I can let Hickory and Dickory run right up my bare arm and sit on my shoulder. Nothing. I don't even twitch. Ask Julie about that. She won't go near them. But that snake really gave me the heebie-jeebies.

Anyway, last Tuesday I did everything right. I washed my hands and face with *hot* water and brushed my teeth *before* eight-thirty. Then I turned out my light and got into bed. That's when I was going to call my parents to come upstairs and kiss me good night.

But Charles, who has a warped sense of humor, wrecked everything.

When I got under my blanket, I felt something slimy with my toe. How could *I* know it wasn't real? It felt exactly real. I mean, if I thought about it, I would have known that old Pea Brain was being tricky again. What my parents don't understand is that it's not so easy to be always *thinking* about things.

Anyway, I screamed, really loud, like on "Creature Feature," and my parents had to come running up the stairs. My mother spilled her coffee on the first night of the tablecloth, and my father ran into the point of the desk. (Which I really don't think was my fault. I mean, he should have *looked* where he was going.) So they were both very mad.

Charles, who *pretended* that he was asleep and that I just woke him, started to cry and make those blubbery sounds of his. He said he never put the snake in my bed, which, for a little kid, was a pretty big lie.

Meanwhile, Blooper had got hold of the snake and was shaking it with his teeth. He

was getting pretty wild, with the screaming and all, and he accidentally knocked the lamp off my night table. My father caught it before it crashed, but he twisted his ankle and said four words that I would be punished for. He should think about *that*.

Now comes the bad part. We went back to sleep, and my mother and father must have gone to sleep, too, because when I woke up the house was dark. A thin line of light was on my carpet and I knew it was from the night-light in the bathroom. The house was scary quiet and I could hear the furniture breathing.

Suddenly I heard a creak, then footsteps coming down the hall. A door closed and the light disappeared from my floor. It was pitch black in my room. I heard the seat cover go up in the bathroom, then fall down and go up again, so I knew it must be Charles. That's when I got my idea.

I got out of bed, very quietly, and tiptoed down the hall to his room. It was very dark and creepy, but I was careful and didn't bunk into anything. Then I got into Charles' bed and pressed myself tight against the wall, so he wouldn't know I was there. I was planning to say "Boo!" and scare him the way he scared me with the snake.

Well, nothing worked out the way I planned it. First of all, Charles' room was pitch, *pitch* black, much blacker than mine. I started to feel really scared, waiting there in the dark. Then I heard the toilet flush and Charles' feet coming back down the hall. I scrunched up as small as I could and held my breath. My heart was beating like a bongo. Charles tripped over something and made a little sound. Then he got into bed.

Right away I knew the whole thing was a mistake. Charles lay down, but I could feel his whole body get stiff, as if he knew something were wrong. I figured I'd better tell him I was there, so I opened my mouth — but stupid Charles stuck his finger in it. Then I bit his finger and we both started to scream. We screamed and screamed. We couldn't stop screaming. We hugged each other so tight, it's a miracle we didn't choke, but we kept on screaming.

Then I heard a crash and my mother's voice wailing, "Oh! Oh! Ohhhhhhh!" and footsteps running down the hall. Then the lights went on and my father was standing there, wrapped in a blanket like an Indian. He looked as if someone had just hit him over the head, and you could tell that his ankle still hurt because he was limping. My mother looked like a pale ghost and when she saw that we weren't dead or anything, she gave a little moan and crumpled onto the floor, like a Kleenex.

Now I know what fainting looks like. It looks very funny if you ask me; and if I hadn't been

so scared, I would have laughed out loud.

The next day my mother didn't look so good and I felt sorry. I thought about what had happened. I thought about it a lot. So I took the snake and put it in a brown paper lunch bag. Then I put the crust from my tuna fish sandwich in the bag, too. Then I threw the bag into the garbage can and stuffed it all the way down to the bottom.

The old Chiperoo didn't even miss it. He had a new black widow spider that he got out of one of those gum machines. This morning I found it hanging on the side of my orange-juice glass. But I didn't scream. As I said, I'm not afraid of spiders.

4

Tomorrow, my mother has to go to school just because Sparky Farentino broke Miss Krinky's glasses during lunchtime.

Annalee Hudder, who everybody hates, told Mrs. Marola, the lunch lady, that David Kretchmar was throwing peas at her. So David had to go down to see The Creep, who is Mr. Cree, our principal.

Annalee is always telling. She's the only

monitor who writes down the name of every single person who talks when Miss Clancy is out of the room.

Miss Clancy is my teacher. She's about seven feet tall and her favorite expression is, "Nobody's perfect." She's always saying how we're all human. I always look over to see if Annalee is listening when she says that.

Annalee is definitely not human. She never gets in trouble and she never gets her smock dirty. Never. Nobody sits next to her on the bus. Once Lillian Mingus sat next to Annalee, but she was new and didn't know any better. Everyone called Lillian cootie, so she never sat next to Annalee again.

Anyway, all the boys at David's table got mad because he was sent to the principal, so they started yelling things like, "Annalee, banana-lee, doesn't have a family!" — which was a dumb thing to say because Gerald Hudder, who

is in seventh grade, plays hockey with Lillian's brother. Also, Mr. Hudder drives in the Sunday School car pool, so everyone knows that Annalee has a family.

Then Eddie Spanbock, who has a big nose and likes to make fun of people, yelled, "Hey, Annalee! Look at me!" He started walking around with his chest stuck out, making believe he was a girl.

Annalee is the only girl in the whole fifth grade who's beginning to grow on top and you could tell she was embarrassed. She wouldn't look at Eddie and she was afraid to get up and tell Mrs. Marola.

Then one of the boys wrote a note and shot it across the room. It landed right in Annalee's mashed potatoes. All the girls started yelling, "Read it, Annalee! What does it say?" but Annalee just sat there, looking down at her plate.

Lillian Mingus grabbed the note and got mashed potatoes all over her fingers. When she shook her hand, a big blob of it flew off and landed on Annalee's blouse. You know where! That cracked everyone up.

Then Annalee went crazy. She picked up a whole handful of potatoes and pushed them in Lillian's face. Lillian looked stupid with her mouth wide open and one eye closed because of the mashed potatoes. She couldn't really see what she was doing, so when she threw her Jell-O at Annalee, it missed her and flew over to our table and hit me in the neck.

I just sat there for a while, with Jell-O dribbling down my neck. Then I picked up my meat loaf and threw it at Lillian.

That's how the whole thing started. Soon the whole cafeteria was throwing food. Kids were putting their whipped-cream topping on their spoons and shooting it at the ceiling, on the walls, everywhere.

Old Thunder Thighs, Mrs. Turtletaub, came charging across the room and got whipped-cream topping right in the middle of her forehead. Miss Bertoli, The Snake, started to hiss,

"Sssssssilence! I want you to ssssstop this racket at once!" And when Miss Krinky, who's about eighty years old, came running to find out what the whole thing was about, she slipped on Sparky Farentino's bread and butter and her glasses flew off her nose and broke.

Miss Krinky, who is practically blind without her glasses, and Annalee, who was hysterical, had to be led out of the cafeteria. Annalee was a wreck. Mrs. Turtletaub kept her arm around her and practically had to carry her out.

The rest of us were sent to The Creep. We lined up in his office and he just stood there, staring at us. He didn't say anything. He just kept pinching his mouth with one hand and staring. We stood like that for a long time. Then his secretary told us to leave and we each got a note to take home.

I couldn't wait to tell Julie. She has lunch

after me and missed the whole thing. I got to the bus late and Julie was sitting near the window, so I sat on the outside, across the aisle from Annalee.

Annalee's eyes were all red and she was pretending to look out the window so no one could see she'd been crying. The seat next to her was empty except for her books. I think she puts them there on purpose so it will look as if she doesn't want anyone sitting next to her.

I began to tell Julie what happened, but she kept saying, "What? *What?*" because I was whispering very low. I gave her my "I'll Tell You Later" look, but Julie, who can be quite dumb, kept saying, "*Tell* me! What *happened?*" I had to jab her with my elbow and kick her in the ankle. Then I wiggled my eyebrows like Groucho Marx and she shut up. I'll have to talk to her about that. She should think more about other people's feelings. I mean, Annalee was right in the next seat.

Julie gets off one stop before me, so I had to get up to let her out. While I was standing, the bus jerked and I fell onto the seat next to Annalee, on top of her books.

I was going to get right up but I didn't. It was only for one stop, anyway, and I figured it would be dumb to change seats. Annalee didn't say anything about me sitting on her books and nobody called me cootie, not even Lillian Mingus.

When we got to my stop, Annalee mumbled something that sounded like good-bye. I wasn't sure, so I said good-bye back, just in case. Then I bunked into Lillian's leg, on purpose, and got off the bus.

I gave the note to my mother after snack so it wouldn't upset my cupcake. Then Julie came over and the lecture had to be postponed.

Tonight, when I was taking my bath, I scrubbed the same spot five times until I saw it was a black-and-blue mark. Then, all of a sudden, out of the clear blue, I thought, "I'm glad I'm not Annalee Hudder."

5

THE WORST PART about Saturday was that I had to get all dressed up. The Chipmunk and I were going into the city to have our pictures taken and I had to wear a blue velvet dress with a white lace collar, and white lace tights that itched my legs.

Friday night my mother set my hair on rollers and Saturday morning she made these big, fat curls all over my head, except on one side where the roller fell out. That place was straight as a stick. My mother had to tuck it behind my ear and pull a curl from the back out in front. I really looked stupid but I didn't think anyone would recognize me, so I didn't make a big fuss. My father said I was a good sport, and Potato Chip, my little brother, snickered with his mouth full of grape juice.

While he was getting his shirt changed, I stood behind my mother and made faces at him. Then I said, "Baby, baby, ha! ha! ha!" — just moving my mouth but not making any sound. That always gets him. He tried to grab me but my mother was hanging on to his shirt, so one of his buttons popped off. My father finally found it under the radiator, and when he stood up his pants were full of cat fur.

That's when my mother made the rules. No more talking. No more moving. No more smiling. No more thinking. We were allowed

to breathe but that was it. The old Chipadee
started taking these loud, deep breaths but he
stopped when my mother gave him one of her
frozen looks. I mean, her eyes got really big

and icy and she stared at him as if he were a Martian or something. Then she clumped back to her room for her other shoe. She is always the last one to get ready.

When we got in the car, Chip had to sit in one corner of the back seat and I had to sit in the other. My mother kept adding new rules all the way over the Fifty-ninth Street Bridge: "Remember! Don't touch each other! Don't speak to each other! Don't even *look* at each other!" I made believe I was turned to stone by a wicked witch, until my neck started to hurt. Then I looked out the window and stuck my tongue out at everyone who looked back at me.

Claude Roger is a very famous photographer. He only takes pictures of children and it was supposed to be a big deal that he was taking pictures of Chippo and me. His studio was on the fifty-ninth floor of a glass building and we had plenty of time to practice good manners going up in the elevator. My mother kept asking if we remembered how to say "How do you do?" — as if we suddenly forgot how to speak or something. Then she thought it would be a good idea if my brother bowed and I curtsied. My father voted against that, which was very lucky, because even if I were *hypnotized* I wouldn't curtsy to anyone! Then my mother arranged my curls for the ten millionth time and my father pulled up Chippee's socks till they were over his knees, and by the time we got to Claude Roger's studio everybody was good and nervous.

Claude Roger is the craziest person I ever met. First of all, you're not supposed to say "Roger," as in "Roger, over and out." You're supposed to say "Roge-*ay*" like the second "*g*" in garage, because he's French. Second of all, he never stopped running, not once, the whole time we were there, which was probably why he was wearing basketball sneakers. He didn't look very famous to me.

The first thing he said when we came in was, *"Sacker bluh!"* which is French and means that he was very upset about something. Then he grabbed a handful of my curls and looked as if he were going to throw up. He kept shaking his head and saying, *"Non, non, non, non, non!"* I thought he was going to yank out my hair and I kept wondering why nobody was stopping him. My mother and father looked as if someone had turned *them* to stone and Chipper, the coward, was hiding behind my father's leg and whispering, "How do you do? How do you do?," like a broken record.

Then this perfect stranger, named Maurice, brushed all the curls out of my hair and Roge-*ay* pulled off Chipper's bow tie and messed up his hair so much you couldn't tell that my

mother had spent one whole hour making his part.

Roge-*ay* explained things to my parents as if they were retards. "Roge-*ay* does not photograph zee ribbons and ruffles!" he told them. "Roge-*ay* does not photograph zee collars and ties! Roge-*ay* wants to know what ees underneath. *Underneath ees zee child!*" Then he yanked open Chippee's collar. I held on to my dress just in case he had any dumb ideas about taking some pictures of my underneath.

Everytime he passed my parents he said, *"Tut, tut, tut, tut, tut!"* in a very disappointed voice. My father looked as though he were going to explode but he never said a word. I think he was afraid of Roge-*ay*. It's funny, too, because he could have beat him up easily.

After a while the Chipmunk and I got to feeling pretty good and it was really something to watch old Twinkle Toes in action. Maurice stood behind a big, black camera, which he aimed at us like a machine gun, and Roge-*ay* skipped around holding a rubber ball that he squeezed whenever he wanted to take our picture. He kept making these crazy faces and asking really dumb questions like: "You are afraid of zee bears, *non?*" or "You are feeling happy, like a red balloon, *wee?*" When we tried to answer he said, "*What? What? What? Eh? Eh? Eh?*" and you could see his gums.

He told the Chipper that if he smiled, really big, he could have a lollipop. I think he fell in love with the hole in Chippee's mouth where his front tooth fell out. He took at least eighty pictures of that hole! Then he didn't give Chip the lollipop, even though he had promised.

I felt sort of bad that all of my front teeth had grown back, so I decided to cross my eyes, which is something the Chipper can't do no matter how hard he tries. Old Gummy Mouth didn't even notice, so I stood in front of the camera and blocked the lens, for a joke.

You never heard so many *non-non-non*s and *tut-tut-tut*s in your life, which proved to me that he may have been a famous photographer but he had a rotten sense of humor! My father gave one of his warning coughs, but Roge-*ay* said good parents were *inveesible* parents, and the coughing stopped. One thing I will say for Roge-*ay*, he really knows how to handle parents. I have to admire him for that.

After some more dumb questions and a lot of running around, the Great Roge-*ay* bounced out of the room and Maurice picked up his hairbrush and told us it was all over.

The minute we got into the elevator my mother whipped out her comb and fixed my hair. Then she put Chippee back together again. I felt like Humpty Dumpty. My father tried to give my mother one of his "Don't Be

Upset" hugs, but she gave him one of her "Don't You Dare Touch Me" looks. Then he said not to look at *him* that way, the whole thing was *her* idea in the first place. After that nobody said anything.

As soon as we got the car started Chipper said, "That man was a big liar and he didn't even *smell* good!" My mother and father laughed as though that were the funniest thing they ever heard. I've told ten times better jokes than that, but they practically got hysterical, so you can't really blame the Chipper. He started hollering, "LIAR! SMELLY LIAR! DUMB, STINKY LIAR! DOPEY, CRAZY LIAR WHO DOESN'T EVEN TELL THE TRUTH!" He was getting funnier by the minute. Then he stood up on the seat and yelled, "STINKY LIAR!" out of all the back windows. He kept stepping on my lap, so I had to give him a good sock to calm him down.

That's when my mother started in with her
rules again. No talking. No touching. No
yelling. No *smirking*!

My father turned on the radio and found a
station that was playing a song called, "Rain-
drops Keep Falling on My Head." He always

sings along to show that he knows all the words.

Pretty soon Chipper fell asleep. His head kept bunking on the side of the car, so I bunched up the front of my coat and made a pillow. I put the old Chipperoo's head on it and straightened out his legs. Then I guess I fell asleep, too, because the next thing I knew, my mother was saying, "Who's hungry?" and we were parked in front of a restaurant that said:

FRESH SEAFOOD

[*]LOBSTERS[*]CRABS[*]SHRIMP[*]CLAMS[*]

Luckily, they had tuna fish, which I had on white bread, with 7-Up and plenty of mayonnaise.

6

GROWN-UPS CAN BE very stupid. I mean *really* stupid. And dumb. Take my Uncle Harvey. When the Chipmunk starts acting impossible, you can blame it on my Uncle Harvey's genes. My mother says that doesn't make any sense because Uncle Harvey is not a blood-relation. He just happens to be married to Aunt Joyce, who is my father's sister. My mother also says that it's rude to say "dumb" and "stupid" about grown-ups, especially relatives. If you ask me, *that* doesn't make any sense. I think people should get what they deserve. Especially relatives.

My Uncle Harvey is in the underwear business and last week he sent me a box of nylon underpants with the days of the week embroidered across the bottoms. I would never wear them. Never. Give me plain old cotton underpants any day. The problem was, I had to write a thank-you note and I couldn't think of anything to say. I thought about it for two days. Then I wrote:

> DEAR UNCLE HARVEY,
>
> I got the underpants you sent me. I never had underpants like that before in my whole life, and I doubt I ever will again. Thank you for thinking about me.

Then I wrote "sincerely" and signed my name. That was on Tuesday.

Sunday was Muzzy's seventy-fifth birthday, so we left the house at about one o'clock and drove to Brooklyn with a present and two bottles of wine. Muzzy is my father's mother. She lives in a brownstone house with two stone lions out front and a big old sun porch in the back. There are eight steps leading to her front door and I can jump from the top step without falling.

My father used to play stoopball on those

steps when he was a little boy. He says there aren't any good stoops on Hummingbird Lane, where we live now. Sometimes, when we're visiting Muzzy, he challenges me to a game of stoopball and Chipper gets to play winners. So far, I won once.

Muzzy lives with my Aunt Eunice, who is my father's oldest sister, and Aunt Eunice's husband, Uncle Polo. Aunt Eunice is skinny as a noodle. My Uncle Harvey says it's because she never had any children. When he says that, my Aunt Joyce always says, "Harvey, why don't you shut up?"

Once, when Uncle Harvey was saying about Aunt Eunice not having any children, my Aunt Joyce was in the bathroom so Chipper said, "Uncle Harvey, why don't you shut up?" Chippee got a slap from my mother and when he tried to explain, my mother put her hand over his mouth. When I grow up, my children will be allowed to say anything that I say. Most of all they will be allowed to speak the TRUTH. Even if it's rude.

When we got to Muzzy's, my father couldn't find a parking space. He had to park two blocks away and as soon as he got out of the car, he stepped in some dog manurc. (That's what I say when I want to be polite.) My father said his usual four words. Then he said something new but I missed most of it. My mother said, "Andrew!" and my father said, "What's the matter with these idiots! Can't they read?"

There was a big sign and I read it to Chip. It said:

CURB YOUR DOG

HELP KEEP OUR CITY CLEAN

Someone had written PLEASE in red paint. I told Chippee what the sign meant and for the next two blocks he kept his eyes glued to the

sidewalk and counted how many dogs had forgotten to read the sign.

When we reached Muzzy's house, he was up to seventeen. Then he asked if he could walk to the corner by himself to see if he could get up to twenty-five. My father yanked his arm so hard that the Chipmunk flew right up to the second step. Then my father took his shoes off and we went inside.

My father has a very big family and everyone was there: Aunt Joyce and Uncle Harvey and Jonathan and Eric and Kevin and Brenda and Aunt Marion and Uncle Rob and Alfred and Barbara and Aunt Cecily and Uncle Caleb and Josh and Sara and Jeremy and Uncle George and Aunt Camille and Wendy and Sharon and Aunt Eunice and Uncle Polo and Muzzy and Mrs. Kaminsky, who is Muzzy's friend from the old country. I had to kiss every single one of them.

I always hate it when I have to kiss a million people. I don't like all of my relatives the same. Some I would rather just shake hands with and some I would like to skip altogether. Like my Uncle Harvey. My cousin Sara, who is one year older than me, feels the same way about it. We are planning a revolution. Some day, when the whole family is there, we're going to walk in and say, "Hi, folks!" Then we're going to march right out to the sun porch, without kissing a single person, and play a game of Monopoly or something.

First I kissed Muzzy. She's soft and wrinkly and she smells of camphor and oranges and cloves. She held my head against her chest and kissed my hair. Then I hugged her very tight and said, "I love you, Muzzy. Happy birthday." My arms could fit around her twice.

My Aunt Camille was puffing on a cigarette, so I had to wait for her to blow out the smoke before I kissed her. Next came Uncle George, who is even worse than Blooper. I had to make believe I had an itch so I could wipe my cheek without him knowing. Then I kissed Aunt Marion. My Aunt Marion never kisses back; she just makes these little kissy sounds with her mouth, as if she's calling a dog. Then she says something like, "It's so nice to see you, Rover." She doesn't *really* say Rover. I just made that up for a joke.

I held my hand over my nose but Uncle Rob pinched it anyway. Then he said, "Hello, Buttercup. Got any new boyfriends?" I said, "Doh, Unca Rob. Dobody doo." He never lets go of my nose until I answer.

Aunt Cecily gave me a great, big hug and whispered, "How's my favorite niece?" I like Aunt Cecily. She's a good hugger. Also, she smells very nice. Then Uncle Caleb picked me up by my elbows and rubbed his beard against my face until it hurt. When I passed Sara, she whispered, "Kissy-kissy," and we both made these suffering faces.

Uncle Polo coughed when I tried to kiss him and his breath smelled like an old cigar. Aunt Eunice was wearing her red pointy shoes. Chippee calls them her "Wicked Witch of the West" shoes. Her hair came to a point on top and she looked exactly like a toothpick. I wonder if a baby could really grow inside of her. If it did, it would have to be very small. About three inches, maybe. Like Thumbalina, or the Liddle Kiddle I got last Christmas. I kissed Aunt Eunice and she smelled like vinegar.

Aunt Joyce was her usual jolly self. She has been jolly ever since the doctor said she was anemic and told her to eat a raw egg every day. At first she gagged a lot. Then someone told her to swallow it down with a mouthful of sherry. Now she has *two* raw eggs a day. My mother says Aunt Joyce is as happy as a clam. She thinks it's because of the eggs. I think it's the sherry. I kissed Aunt Joyce and she kissed me back.

I always save Uncle Harvey for last. Not because he's the best, but because I always hope he'll get an important phone call and have to leave before I get to him. So far that never happened. As soon as I got near Uncle Harvey, he picked up my dress and shouted, "WHAT DAY IS IT, SWEETHEART?"

Everybody laughed. I could have punched him right in his fat stomach. I grabbed my dress and tried to think of something to say. Something mean that would embarrass him. Something that would make him stop laughing and shut his big mouth. "Why don't you buy a calendar, Uncle Harvey?" I said, and everybody burst out laughing again.

I hate it when I'm going to cry. I have to make a fist and bite my cheek. My Aunt Joyce said, "Your Uncle Harvey didn't mean anything. To him you're still a baby. Besides, what's a pair of panties between friends?"

One thing about grown-ups, they always stick together. I asked my Aunt Joyce, "How would you like it if someone picked up your dress in front of everybody?" and when she didn't answer I said, "Think about it. You might learn something!"

What I would like to do is learn to embroider. Then the next time Uncle Harvey picks up my dress and says, "WHAT DAY IS IT, SWEET-HEART?" it would say in big red letters, right across the bottom of my underpants: UNCLE HARVEY, WHY DON'T YOU SHUT UP! Also, I wish he would stop calling me sweetheart!!

The rest of the day was okay. Muzzy had a giant cake with about two million candles on it, and we all blew them out together. I got a piece with a pink rose, and two scoops of pistachio ice cream.

When we sang "Happy Birthday" Muzzy looked as though she were going to cry. Everybody hollered, "SPEECH! SPEECH!" and Muzzy said, "Next year, with God's help, we'll all be together again and you can wish me another happy birthday." Then everyone clapped and shouted "HOORAY!" and Josh, who is a hippy, yelled, "Right on, Muzzy!"

Later, Uncle Harvey pinched my cheek and said, "Hey, sweetheart. How about you and me being friends?" I said okay, even though I wasn't really finished being angry. Sometimes Uncle Harvey isn't *that* bad.

When it was time to leave, all the grandchildren got a honey cake to take home. Not big ones, but really neat small ones that Muzzy baked herself with almonds all over the top.

One think I know. I love Muzzy. I don't even have to think about that.

7

I THOUGHT A LOT about inviting Annalee Hudder but she didn't have a sleeping bag. That's how I decided. Everyone who was invited to my sleep-in had to have a sleeping bag.

It was my idea to call it a sleep-in. Pajama party sounded too immature. Also, Fern Pollinger, who combs her hair seventy-eight times a day, had a pajama party last May.

I planned it for Monday, December 23. There was no school the next day because of winter recess, which used to be called Christmas vacation but was changed so that everyone would be included. I think that was a pretty good idea.

In our house we celebrate Chanukah *and* Christmas. We also celebrate Thanksgiving, Halloween, Passover, the Fourth of July, St. Patrick's Day, and the Chinese New Year.

Miss Clancy, my teacher, says we are children of the universe. My mother says that, as a child of the universe, I should have invited Annalee Hudder. Even after I *explained* to her about the sleeping bag.

Lillian Mingus and Grace Bishop had sleeping bags from summer camp. Julie and I had ours from Girl Scouts, and Fern had a purple one with pink flowers all over it from Lord & Taylor's. And a nightgown to match.

Julie and I made the invitations about a week in advance. She said she wanted to get one even though she was helping to make them, so we drew four sleeping bags on red construction paper and cut them out with my mother's poultry shears. I didn't even ask what happened to the regular scissors because of how my mother gets when anything is missing.

Next, we wrote this poem:

Come to a sleep-in on Hummingbird Lane.
Come if it's snowing.
Come if it rains.
Come with your sleeping bag.
Wear your old jeans.
Supper's at six and it's hot dogs and beans.

P.S. Breakfast is included.

We weren't really going to have hot dogs and beans, but Julie and I couldn't think of

anything to rhyme with pizza. I figured everyone would be surprised.

It took one whole day to make the invitations. We had to write very small to get the
whole poem on one side of the sleeping bag.
I got a little tuna fish on mine and Julie ripped
hers from erasing so much, so we had to do
them twice. My mother wanted us to say that
the whole thing would be over the next morning
at 11 A.M. sharp. She is always hinting, which
she calls "making suggestions."

At the last minute we remembered that we
didn't put in the date, so we had to print
Monday, December 23, on the envelopes. Then
we mailed them. We even mailed Julie's.

Sunday night it snowed and Monday morning
I was the first one up. Snitch gets nervous when
it's too deep, but Blooper and I love the snow.
We went outside and rolled around in it and
I made an angel. Then I made a snowman,

but Blooper peed on it. Mr. Hennesy, the milkman, thought that was very funny.

When we came inside, I wiped Blooper's feet off, almost perfect. Later, my father came downstairs and we had breakfast together. I cooked the whole thing myself. The important

thing about making hot cakes is to put in lots and lots of butter so they won't stick. My father said they were out of this world and the only reason he couldn't finish all of them was because it was getting so late. Luckily, I remembered that his right boot was in the box where my mother saves the shopping bags, or he would have missed *two* trains.

My Aunt Cecily came over in the afternoon to get Chipper, who was going to sleep at her house. He took his blue blanket and his black widow spider with him and, before he left, he made me swear on the dictionary that I'd save him a strawberry cupcake. I always swear on the dictionary because it doesn't count, but I saved him a cupcake anyway.

Julie came over early. Her pajamas and stuff were rolled up in her sleeping bag and the whole thing was strapped onto her back. She looked really neat, as if she were in college.

When we grow up we're going to travel around together. All over the world, especially Paris and Africa.

We called up Lillian and told her to come early, too. Then the three of us made a cave in the snow, behind the garage, and talked about what we should do at the sleep-in. Julie thought we should have entertainment. She wanted to make up a dance routine, but it was too hard practicing with our boots on and no one felt like going inside.

Lillian thought we should sing a women's liberation song. We both knew the words. The only problem was Julie. Every time we came to the part that goes, "I am strong. I am invincible!" Julie would sing, "I am strong. I am *invisible!*"

Lillian kept shouting, "You're missing the whole *point!*" and we had to do it over about eighty-nine times until Julie got it right.

Grace and Fern came over at five-thirty and we unrolled our sleeping bags in the living room. Fern even had a bathrobe to match her sleeping bag, *and* purple fluffies. She must have thought it was going to be a regular fashion show or something.

The sleep-in was really fantastic. Nobody got bored. Julie didn't say *invisible* and my parents didn't get upset. Not even when Grace spilled her black-raspberry soda all over Fern's sleeping bag. Lucky for Fern, most of it went into her fluffy.

Later, we played I Packed My Grandmother's Trunk and Lillian won every single time. She must have one of those *photogenic* memories. But — and it's not because I'm jealous or anything — she is a rotten winner. I mean Lillian is not exactly what you would call humble. Every time she won, she would clap her hands and make these *honking* sounds, like a regular seal. Grace must have thought so, too, because one time she said, "Does anybody have a *fish?*" I was the only one who caught on so I raised my left eyebrow, which is something I have been practicing, to let her know that at least one other person got the joke. Grace really has a terrific sense of humor. She could be a comedian if she wanted to.

We also played Ghost and Charades. I am

really fantastic when it comes to Charades, and that's not bragging. That's the truth. Ask anyone. Fern thinks I should be an actress but I don't know what I want to be. I think it's dumb to make up your mind ahead of time. I want to be everything.

Later on, we all went up to my room to get into our pajamas. Everybody felt sort of embarrassed to get undressed but nobody wanted to admit it. We all pretended that we didn't care. Grace said how we were all girls anyway, and Fern said it was really dumb to be shy. Then she said that she had to go to the bathroom. She took her nightgown with her.

The rest of us got undressed really fast, then I said, "Last one in her sleeping bag's a rotten egg," and we all raced down the stairs.

At 11 o'clock (which I thought was too early) my mother and father turned out the lights. It felt funny to be sleeping in the living room,

on the floor. I could see the moon through the windows, and the stars.

We stayed up for hours, just talking and fooling around. Most of the time we remembered to whisper but Fern has this really crazy laugh, like a hyena with cramps, and my father finally banged on the floor and hollered down that some people had to go to *work* in the morning.

Fern thought that was hysterically funny and I had to put my pillow over her head to shut her up. Then Blooper started to bark and the sleep-in was almost wrecked, but Julie noticed that it was snowing again and everyone calmed down.

It was the fat kind of snow. Perfect for snowballs. Lillian started to sing "Frosty the Snowman" and we all joined in. Then we sang Christmas carols, very softly.

When we got to the part that goes, "Peace

on earth, good will to men," I remembered that I once read, "Peace on earth, good will to *people.*" That means everybody. I thought about that for a while, then I fell asleep with Blooper on my stomach.

8

It's THREE O'CLOCK in the morning and the reason I'm not sleeping is because Mrs. Grundy, also known as The Enchanted Ear, is downstairs in the living room watching The Early Early Movie. The TV is turned up so loud that even the people in China must be going deaf. It sounds like one of those dumb love stories where Ethel loves Bill and Bill loves Mona. I can tell because of the way everyone is screaming and carrying on.

It's always the same in those movies. The troublemaker has wild blond hair and her name ends with an "a," like Mona, or Lolita, or Veronica. People named Ethel, or Margaret, or Shirley have neat hair and never make any trouble, which would probably be a good thing to remember.

Anyway, Ethel must have just walked in and found Bill kissing Mona, because it sounds as if the whole violin section of the New York Philharmonic Symphony Orchestra is playing downstairs in my living room. Ethel is screaming, "OH BILL, HOW CAN YOU DO THIS TO ME!" and Mona is screaming, "BILL DARLING, I LOVE YOU!" Bill is just screaming. Period.

Mrs. Grundy has been glued to the television set for at least eight hours. I would have been bored to death an hour ago. In my whole life, I never sat and watched television for so long.

Not even when I had the chicken pox, with complications, and had to stay in bed for over a week.

Mrs. Gertrude Grundy is our baby sitter when we can't get anyone else. She is about seven hundred years old and half-deaf, but she pretends that she can hear everything. Even a pin dropping two thousand miles away, which

is why Chippee and I call her The Enchanted Ear.

Whenever she sees us whispering, she starts acting like the FBI and the CIA all rolled into one. She also makes these suspicious little remarks, like, "Never mind making any of your plans when I'm around. I can hear every word you're saying!" She must think we're secret agents, planning to blow up the whole world.

The trouble with Mrs. Grundy is that she doesn't trust anybody. She's always snooping around after us and hollering up the stairs, "WHAT ARE YOU CHILDREN DOING UP THERE? I KNOW YOU'RE UP TO SOME-THING! YOU CAN'T FOOL ME!"

Sometimes, just to trick her, Chippo tells Blooper to speak. Then, as soon as he barks, Mrs. Grundy hollers up, "I CAN HEAR EVERY SINGLE WORD, SO NONE OF YOUR LITTLE TRICKS!" That really cracks us up.

We also like to pop out of the closet and scare her.

My mother and father always ask us to be extra nice to her because she lives all alone and doesn't have any family, but there's something about Mrs. Grundy that makes me act rotten even when I want to act nice. It's sort of like the way I am with Annalee Hudder, only for different reasons. I really have to think about that.

The reason why Mrs. Grundy is downstairs watching television at three o'clock in the morning in the first place, is because it's New Year's Eve and my parents haven't come home yet. It's a good thing that nobody has to go to work tomorrow morning.

I can hardly wait till I'm old enough to stay up until 3 A.M. in front of people. First of all, it's very hard to write in this notebook and hold my flashlight steady at the same time.

Second of all, I can hardly breathe underneath the blanket. Third of all, it's very bad for my eyes. Mrs. Grundy probably knows all that, but she's too lazy to climb the stairs and take away my flashlight. Anyway, I doubt she would care even if my eyes fell out.

My mother would say I'm feeling sorry for myself. She says when people feel sorry for themselves, even angels have horns. My mother says these very deep things when she wants to make a point. Sometimes, by the time I figure out what she means, I forget what we were talking about. But she would be right. I am feeling sorry for myself. But I have a very good reason.

I thought it would be a terrific idea if the four of us celebrated New Year's together. Just my mother and father, and Chippee, and me, with hors d'oeuvres and popcorn and fancy stuff like that. I figured we could play Charades or Monopoly, and it would be a real treat for the Chipper since he hardly gets to go to any parties. But my parents have this thing about New Year's Eve. My mother thinks she'll get hives or something if she stays home. At least that's how she acts. Every year she says how stupid it is for people to make such a big fuss over New Year's, but all the time she's saying how stupid it is, she's zooming in and out of the stores looking for something new to wear.

When I grow up I will never be like that. I will never do things that I think are stupid. I will stay home with my children and give them champagne and popcorn, and at midnight we'll clink our glasses and say "Happy New Year" together. I certainly won't leave them with a boring person like Mrs. Grundy, who just sits around and watches TV all night.

Mrs. Grundy didn't look as though she were

having such a good time either, so, when we remembered what my parents said about being nice to her, Chippo and I snuck some pots and pans upstairs with us at bedtime and set the alarm for five minutes to twelve. Then, at exactly midnight, we marched downstairs to the living room, banging away on the pots and yelling, "HAPPY NEW YEAR, MRS. GRUNDY!" — just to spark her up a little. It really worked. You could tell. She even screamed, she was so excited. That's probably what they mean about screaming for joy. She even forgot to tell us she could hear every single word we were saying, which is pretty funny when you think about it.

After I brought her a glass of water, Chippee and I went back upstairs and I tucked him into bed. Then we said what we would like to be if we could be anything we wanted. Chipper wants to be a magic giant, which I tried to

talk him out of because giants don't have any friends, and besides they're too big. But Chippee said giants have diamond refrigerators, so it doesn't matter if they have any friends or not. I couldn't think of anything to say to that, so I just said good night and went back to my own room.

I have been trying to fall asleep for almost three hours but the television keeps waking me up. I don't mind too much because I want to be up when my parents come home. They always bring home horns and party hats, and I'm really starting to miss them a lot.

My radio-alarm clock has numbers that light up in the dark and it feels as if I'm watching the whole night go by. When I wake up in the morning (if I ever fall asleep), it will be the first day of a new year. I think this will be the last chapter in my notebook. It's all used up anyway, just like this year, so tomorrow I'm going to start out fresh.

Aunt Cecily and Uncle Rob gave me a really great book for Christmas. It has a cover that looks like real leather, and it's blue, and there's a fourteen-carat gold line all around the border. It's not exactly a book because all the pages are empty and there are no words on the cover telling what's inside. It doesn't say "My Five Year Diary," or "My Sketch Book," or "My Photograph Album." Nothing like that. I mean, I can write stories, or draw pictures, or just sort things out. I can even scribble in it if I want to, which would be pretty stupid, but it's up to me. My mother says it has possibilities.

Possibilities is a word I like. I mean, you don't find many things with possibilities these days. Everything has a label. Like jars that say COOKIES or FLOUR, and boxes that say LOLLIPOPS FOR GOOD LITTLE GIRLS AND BOYS, or some dumb thing like that — always telling you what to do.

I have this five-gallon fish tank, with a crack in it, that I bought for twenty-five cents at the Salvation Army. Once I put a bird's nest and an almost perfect blue egg in it. Another time I put in a whole bunch of milkweed and seven striped caterpillars. I was going to watch the caterpillars turn themselves into butterflies, which would have been a good idea, except someone left the cover off the tank. I told my mother not to worry because the caterpillars would come back as soon as they got hungry, but she worried anyway. She said she couldn't decide if she wanted them to get found or stay lost. It worked out that five of them stayed lost. Snitch found the other two.

It's all really the same thing. My fish tank, and my new book, and this brand-new year. They all have possibilities. I think it's pretty exciting. I mean, you can really think about that.

Jennifer West